THIS **ELEPHANT & PIGGIE** BOOK
BELONGS TO:

_____

_____

_____

To my friend Alessandra

Today I Will Fly!

By **Mo Willems**

WALKER BOOKS
AND SUBSIDIARIES
LONDON · BOSTON · SYDNEY · AUCKLAND

An **ELEPHANT & PIGGIE** Book

Today I will fly!

No.

You will not fly today.

You will not fly
next week.

She will not fly.

Fly, fly, fly, fly, fl

y, fly, fly, fly, fly!

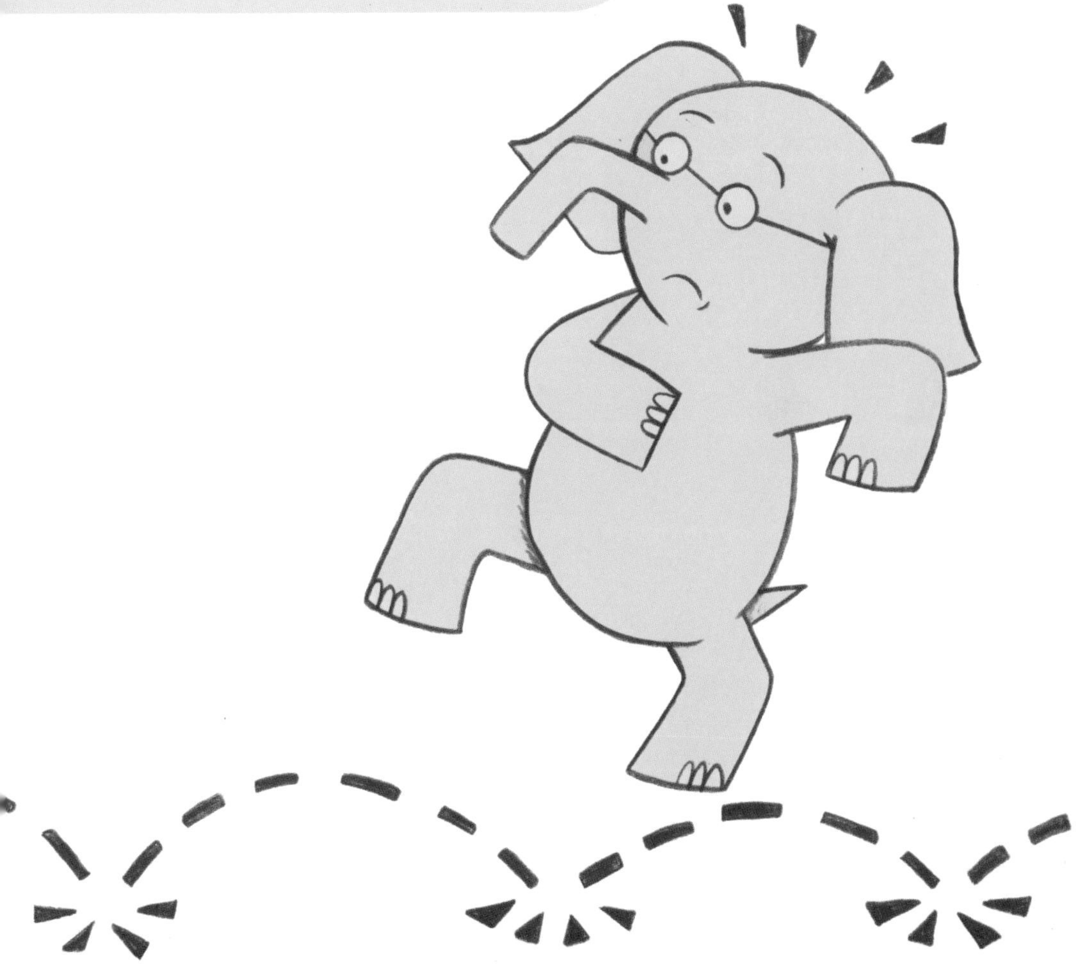

Fly, fly, fly, fly!

You need help.

I will get help!

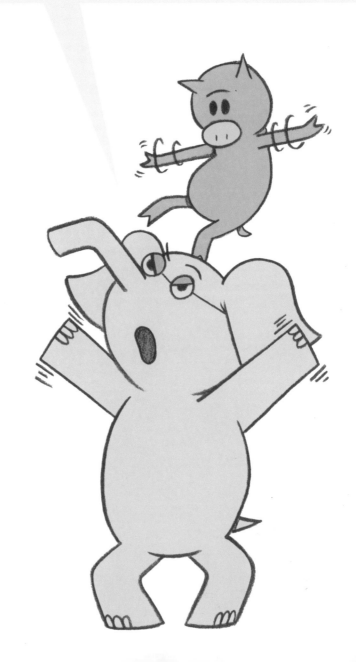

31

Yes, it was a big jump.
But you did not fly.

33

I will eat lunch.

Goodbye!

Fly! Fly! Fly!

You need help.

Will you help me?

I will.
I will help you.

Thank you.

Hello?

Hello!

You are flying today!

My friend can fly!
She can fly!

I am *not* flying!

50

I am getting help.

Thank you for your help!

Tomorrow *I* will fly!

Mo Willems is the author of the Caldecott Honor-winning books
Knuffle Bunny: A Cautionary Tale and *Don't Let the Pigeon Drive the Bus!*
His other groundbreaking picture books include *Leonardo, the Terrible Monster*
and *Edwina, the Dinosaur Who Didn't Know She Was Extinct*.

Mo began his career as a writer and animator on *Sesame Street*,
where he garnered six Emmy Awards.

This is a work of fiction. Names, characters, places and incidents are either
the product of the author's imagination or, if real, are used fictitiously.

First published in Great Britain 2008 by Walker Books Ltd
87 Vauxhall Walk, London SE11 5HJ

2 4 6 8 10 9 7 5 3

© 2007 Mo Willems

First published in the United States by Hyperion Books for Children
British publication rights arranged with Sheldon Fogelman Agency, Inc.

The right of Mo Willems to be identified as author and illustrator of this work has been
asserted by him in accordance with the Copyright, Designs and Patents Act 1988

This book has been typeset in Century 725 and Grilled Cheese

Printed in Singapore

British Library Cataloguing in Publication Data:
a catalogue record for this book is available from the British Library

ISBN 978-1-4063-1467-0

www.walkerbooks.co.uk

www.pigeonpresents.com